THE WARLOCK'S STAFF

TorpiX
THE TWISTING
SERPENT

With special thanks to
J.N. Richards

For my cousins Jayden and Lucas

www.beastquest.co.uk

ORCHARD BOOKS
338 Euston Road, London NW1 3BH
Orchard Books Australia
Level 17/207 Kent St, Sydney, NSW 2000

A Paperback Original
First published in Great Britain in 2011

Beast Quest is a registered trademark of Beast Quest Limited
Series created by Beast Quest Limited, London

A CIP catalogue record for this book is available from
the British Library.

ISBN 978 1 40831 321 3

3 5 7 9 10 8 6 4

Printed in Great Britain by CPI Group (UK) Ltd, Croydon, CR0 4YY

The paper and board used in this paperback are natural recyclable
products made from wood grown in sustainable forests. The
manufacturing processes conform to the environmental regulations of
the country of origin.

Orchard Books is a division of Hachette Children's Books,
an Hachette UK company

www.hachette.co.uk

TORPIX
THE TWISTING SERPENT

BY ADAM BLADE

ORCHARD

Tom and Elenna are such fools! They thought their Quests were over and that my master was defeated. They were wrong! For now Malvel has the Warlock's Staff, hewn from the Tree of Being, and all kingdoms will soon be at his mercy.

We travel the land of Seraph, to find the Eternal Flame. And when we burn the Staff in the flame, our evil magic will be unstoppable. Tom and Elenna can chase us if they wish, but they'll find more than just Beasts lying in wait. They're alone this time, with no wizard to help them.

I hope Tom and Elenna are ready to meet me again. I've been waiting a long time for my revenge.

Yours, with glee, Petra the Witch

PROLOGUE

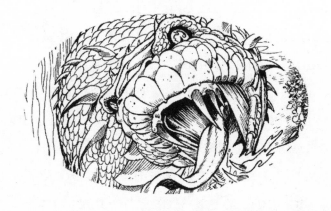

Malvel took in a ragged breath and leant heavily on the Warlock's Staff. The air was thin on the mountain ledge. Every part of his body ached from the long climb up the steep rocky path and his legs felt like they were made from lead.

The Dark Wizard scowled. His body had become so feeble!

But it won't be for long, he reminded himself. *Once I reach the Eternal Flame and put the Warlock's Staff in the magical fire, I'll be strong again.* Malvel's face twisted into an evil grin. "I will be the most powerful wizard in all the known kingdoms," he rasped.

Malvel cackled but quickly began to wheeze and cough. He wiped a hand across his mouth and struggled on higher up the mountain, his bones creaking. Sweat stung his eyes and the wind whipped at his robes, but still the Dark Wizard climbed.

Soon he reached the top of the rocky wall and found himself standing on a vast plateau. It was barren except for a hedge of thickly twisted green vines that grew a head taller than he stood. The vines were as thick as his arms and looked shiny and tough. Malvel's heart leapt. Through the tiny gaps in the vines, he could see a vibrant orange glow – the Eternal Flame.

I've finally made it!

Finding new strength in his tired legs, Malvel rushed forwards.

He scanned the hedge, searching for a place where he could wriggle through. But the thick vines were knotted together too tightly. The huge plant looked like a tangled fishing net.

Malvel frowned. Were the vines enchanted to protect the flame? His fingers found the carved stick at his waist. "The magic of the Warlock's Staff may help me," he muttered.

Raising the staff above his head, Malvel plunged it into a tiny gap between two vines.

A hole appeared, an arm-span wide. Dark, menacing smoke curled from its edges. As swiftly as his old body would allow, Malvel clambered through and tumbled across the earth on the other side. The vines hissed angrily. The black smoke was blasted away by a powerful wind. Malvel dropped the Warlock's Staff to the ground and the hole quickly closed up again.

Malvel struggled to his feet and felt a shiver of excitement go through his body. In front of him stood the Eternal Flame! The fire flared high but did not flicker or splutter, despite the fierce winds.

Malvel stepped towards it cautiously, expecting to feel a gust of heat slap his face – but the flame did not give off any warmth at all.

Magic fire! Malvel thought with wonder. *Powerful enough to make me the ruler of every kingdom.* He advanced slowly, walking right up to it.

As he peered more closely, two bright eyes appeared. Malvel took a step back in surprise as a huge snake rose from the cold flames.

Stupid, stupid! he cursed himself. In his eagerness to reach the Eternal Flame he hadn't stopped to think whether a Beast might be here!

Malvel felt the hairs on his arms

stand on end as the serpent reared up
to its full height. The snake was as
tall as an oak and its red and yellow
scales glinted in the light of the fire.
Along its back, scales rose like spikes.
The giant Beast opened its mouth
wide and Malvel could see venom
glistening on its fangs. The Dark
Wizard wanted to move but fear
froze him to the spot.

The snake hissed and a jet of yellow
acid flew from its mouth, landing on
Malvel's cloak. The Dark Wizard
screamed as the acid burnt through
and seared his skin.

He leapt back and threw off the
cloak, his heart pounding.

The snake lunged for him but
Malvel jerked to his left, managing
to roll out of the way just in time,
although his tired body screamed in

protest. He crawled towards the vines on his hands and his knees.

"I must get away. I must get away," Malvel whispered.

Something slapped around his ankles. Looking over his shoulder he could see that the snake's tongue had wrapped around his feet. It felt like a rope of flames had him caught, as acid from the snake's tongue burnt through to his skin.

Malvel screamed as he was lifted off the ground, spinning in the air as the Beast snapped his tongue back and brought the wizard towards his mouth. The Beast's breath was hot on Malvel's face.

With a hoarse cry the Dark Wizard lifted the Warlock's Staff and brought it down on the Beast's head with a crack. The snake hissed in pain and his tongue unravelled – releasing Malvel. The Staff flew out of Malvel's hand and it spun through the air, landing on the other side of the vines.

I'm doomed! Malvel thought, as the snake's tongue darted out to curl around his body.

He heard a cackle of laughter. Looking down he saw a familiar stout figure approaching the Staff that lay unguarded on the ground...

"Petra!" Malvel growled at his apprentice. "Leave that Staff alone! It's mine!"

Petra grinned up at him. "Quiet, old man. You can't tell me what to do. Now *I* have the Warlock's Staff."

"Traitor!" Malvel screamed as he was dragged towards the snake's mouth.

"And you're about to become

a snake's supper," Petra replied
holding the Staff above her head.

The little witch's smug face was
the last thing Malvel saw before the
Beast's mouth closed around him.

CHAPTER ONE

THE DIAMOND TUNNELS

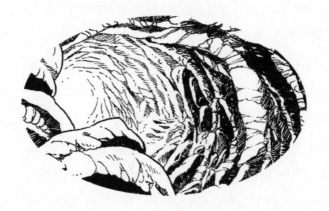

"Do you think the Eternal Flame is near?" Elenna asked. Her voice sounded hollow and ghostly as it echoed off the walls of the damp tunnels that lay beneath Seraph.

"I hope so," Tom murmured. "The future of every kingdom depends on it."

Varra, the leader of the Seraph

fishing village, had told Tom that the
tunnels were a shortcut to the
Eternal Flame, but he was still
worried. He and Elenna had to get to
the flame before Malvel brought the
Warlock's Staff to the fire, or the
Dark Wizard would gain power over
all the known kingdoms, including
Avantia. Tom frowned as he thought
of how Malvel and Petra had been
criss-crossing the kingdom on their
way to the Eternal Flame, using evil
magic to turn the innocent creatures
and people of Seraph into Beasts.

It had not been easy, but Tom had
managed to undo their evil magic at
each stage of his Quest. He smiled as
he remembered his most recent
victory. He had restored a mighty
sea Beast called Spikefin to his
original human form.

My Quest hasn't just been about defeating Malvel, Tom thought, feeling a spurt of anxiety. *It's also about saving Aduro's life.* The Good Wizard had collapsed and disappeared at the start of this Quest because Malvel had stolen the Warlock's Staff. Without the Staff in its rightful place in King Hugo's palace, Aduro had become weak and melted away. Tom was determined to return the Staff. Nothing would stop him from helping his friend!

Tom and Elenna walked on, leading Storm and Silver through the tunnels. Tom could feel his stallion dragging his hooves, while Silver the wolf stayed close to Elenna's side and made low whining noises.

Tom didn't blame his animal friends for being nervous. The tunnels were

dark and the air felt heavy with
menace. This place made the hairs
on his arm stand on end.

"Tom! Look!" Elenna said, pointing
to a glimmer of light ahead.

"It's the way out!" Tom exclaimed.

"It has to be."

The four friends hurried forwards, turning a corner. Tom stopped as a flood of bright light surrounded them. Squinting against the glare, he looked around to see…

"Diamonds!" Elenna gasped.

They were everywhere. A wall of glittering jewels reared up from the ground and crusted the tunnel's ceiling. Every surface was covered with a sparkling white glow that seemed to come from the heart of the diamonds.

"I don't understand," Elenna said. "They must be reflecting light – but where's it coming from?"

Tom glanced around. There wasn't a single beam of sunlight or the glow of a candle. He gingerly placed a hand against one of the diamond-encrusted walls. It felt warm and pulsed under his palm. "It must be some kind of magic," he said. "At least now we can see properly where we're going." Whatever magic this was, Tom felt glad of it.

They walked on through the diamond tunnel. The path began to slant steeply upwards, and the slippery, diamond-encrusted ground beneath Tom's feet made it difficult to keep his balance.

With a high-pitched whinny of fear, Storm reared up on his hind legs and kicked out, slipping backwards.

"Whoa, boy!" Tom ducked under Storm's flailing hooves and wrapped the horse's bridle around his hand. He planted his feet and pulled, the muscles in his arms straining as he yanked on the bridle so that the stallion didn't slide any further back. A horse with a broken leg would be a disaster this far underground.

Storm's hooves clattered back onto the diamond floor but his sides were heaving and his mouth flecked with foam.

Tom stroked Storm's mane soothingly. "What's the matter, boy?"

"He's scared of the reflections," Elenna said, kneeling to stroke her wolf's bristling fur. "So is Silver."

Tom looked around him. They were surrounded by their reflections in every direction. Distorted images of the four of them flickered and danced on the shiny diamond walls and stretched out across the roof of the tunnel.

Tom felt sweat prickle on his skin. The longer he looked, the more sinister and distorted the reflections became. Every flicker of movement on the diamond wall looked like a potential attacker. *Perhaps this isn't good magic, after all*, he thought – although he didn't dare say the words out loud.

"We should go, now!" Elenna jumped to her feet. "Can't you feel it? It's like we're being watched… And the walls…they're pressing in on us!"

Tom drew his sword and swiped it in front of him in an arc, ready to defend his friends. But nothing leapt forward and the walls did not move.

"Elenna, stay calm," Tom said. "The light from the diamonds is making you see things."

Elenna raked a hand through her short hair. "I don't understand, I could have sworn that those walls were moving."

"Come on," Tom said. "We have to find a way out of here." The sooner they were back at ground level, the better. They had a Quest to complete!

Elenna nodded, straightening her shoulders. "You're right, let's go."

Tom smiled to himself as Elenna strode forward, leading the way. Silver lolloped by her side and Storm followed closely behind. Tom and his friends soon fell into a slow and steady pace.

Elenna froze and Silver almost collided with her.

"What's wrong?" Tom called. "Are you alright?"

His friend gave a choked scream. "I was right. The walls are moving in on us!" she gasped. "We've got to get out of here!" She broke into a run, with Silver following. Storm had already pushed ahead, neighing nervously.

Tom could hear a slow, grinding noise like stone scraping across stone. Or diamonds scraping across diamonds! He looked around himself, turning in a tight circle. Elenna was right. Slowly but surely the glittering walls of the tunnel were sliding closer and closer. He turned to follow his friends, but the ground beneath his feet began to rumble. He heard a creaking sound from above – the ceiling was descending, too.

He felt a sudden sharp pain in his arm and glanced down. A jutting shard of diamond was slowly beginning to press into his flesh, its sharp point cutting through Tom's tunic.

Elenna had been right.

Why hadn't Tom moved more quickly?

We're going to be crushed! he thought.

CHAPTER TWO

TRAPPED!

"Elenna, run!" Tom yelled. He tried to move forward but his sleeve was pinned to the opposite wall by the blade of diamond and his arm was caught. He had to turn his body sideways to avoid being crushed. Luckily, Storm was already ahead, just beyond the moving tunnel walls.

Tom tugged at his sleeve, but the fabric refused to tear. He looked desperately at his friend. "I can't move. You've got to save yourself and get out of the tunnel."

Elenna shook her head stubbornly. "I'm not leaving you."

She reached forwards through the narrow gap and grabbed his arm. Silver ran over, squeezing through, and sank his teeth into the material of Tom's trousers, while Storm thrust his head forwards so that his bridle dangled into Tom's hands. Still, there was the relentless grinding sound of the walls closing in.

"Tom, get ready and hold onto Storm's bridle," Elenna shouted. "This might hurt."

Gritting her teeth and bracing her feet against the slippery diamond floor, Elenna tugged with all her might. Silver shoved his body against

the back of Tom's legs and Storm
reared back, pulling on the bridle.
Tom heard the material of his tunic
tear and then felt a flash of pain as
the diamond cut into his skin.
Warm blood trickled down his arm.

Tom gritted his teeth and shut his
mind to the pain as the diamond
dragged across his skin. Then, with
one final tug, he was free! He
staggered forward and felt a wave
of relief.

That was close, he thought. Tom
slapped a hand to the wound on his
arm, putting pressure on it to stop
the blood welling up. Behind them,
the walls were still closing in.

"Are you all right?" Elenna asked.

"I'm fine, it's only a scratch," Tom
said with a smile at Silver and Storm.
"Thanks for saving me. All of you."

Elenna shrugged. "Anytime. It's what friends are for, isn't it? Come on, we need to keep moving."

They hurried through the tunnel. Tom held onto Storm's bridle as Silver led the way. The wolf growled at something near the top of the tunnel.

Tom peered ahead and saw the silhouette of a squat girl with greasy hair. Petra, Malvel's apprentice! Her reflection was thrown up on the glittering tunnel walls.

"What do you want?" Tom asked.

"I'm here to help you," Petra said, her voice echoing off the diamond walls. "I know a way out of here. Just follow me."

Tom and Elenna shared a doubtful look.

"Why should we trust you?"

Elenna asked. "The last time we saw
you, you left us to drown."

The witch shrugged. "Suit yourself
– let these walls crush you like a nut.
That's what they do to those who
seek the Eternal Flame." She turned
to leave as the grinding sound grew
louder. Now, this part of the tunnel
was closing in on them! Tom felt the
ground rumbling under his feet. He

wasn't going through that again.

"Wait," Tom said quickly. "We're coming."

"Tom, no, we shouldn't," Elenna said. "She'll betray us again."

"We don't have much choice," said Tom. His fingers crept to the sword by his side. He knew the young witch could not be trusted. "I'll be on my guard," he told his friend in a quiet voice. "You can trust me, at least."

Elenna looked uncertain, then gave a nod. "Come on, then."

They followed Petra through a maze of tunnels. Tom was grateful that she didn't try to talk to them as they walked. Eventually they saw a circle of light ahead of them. It became bigger with each step that they took.

"The exit from the tunnel," Petra

said as they drew closer. "I told you
I could be trusted."

"We'll see about that," Tom replied.
Then he whispered to Elenna: "Stay
alert. Who knows what will be
waiting for us on the other side?"

Elenna nodded and Tom drew his
sword as they reached the tunnel
entrance.

They emerged high up in the
mountains on a vast plateau that was
almost barren except for a towering
hedge of twisted, thick vines that
looked as smooth as polished glass.
The sky above was clear blue, but
a fierce wind drove across the
mountaintop.

Tom scanned the exposed ground,
expecting an ambush at any moment.
There was no one in sight. Below
them stretched the kingdom of

Seraph. It was many days' ride away, but the green meadows and fields of golden crops looked as beautiful as ever. Thanks to Tom, there were no Beasts roaming in the valleys below. *But up here?* Tom thought, his glance quickly sailing over the nearby rocks and windswept trees. *At every stage of this Quest, I've met an enemy. There's sure to be one here too*, he reminded himself. He couldn't afford to relax for a moment.

Petra pointed at the vines and took a step towards them. "The Eternal Flame lies beyond these."

"Why are you helping us, Petra?" Tom demanded. The sound of his voice was almost whipped away by the wind. "The last time we met, you hit me over the head and sent me over a waterfall."

"I'm sorry, I was wrong to do that," Petra said, casting her eyes downward. "Being Malvel's apprentice warped my mind. It takes me a long time to trust people."

Tom stared at the witch – she

looked genuinely sorry, but he still couldn't allow himself to trust her.

"All right, I won't try to fight you," he said. "But keep your distance. You need to earn our trust."

Petra's face formed a frown, but then her brow cleared. "As you say," she muttered.

Tom led the way towards the vines and the others followed. Elenna kept an arrow trained on Petra.

Tom's grip tightened on his sword. *If the Eternal Flame really lies behind these twisted plants, then where is Malvel?* Tom asked himself. *Have we really got to the fire before the Dark Wizard?*

Tom stabbed the blade of his sword into the stony earth, dug into his pocket and took out his tapestry map. There was no sign of what the next

Beast looked like. But there was an etching of the Beast's name – Torpix. *What type of Beast will it be?* Tom wondered. *Had it already met Malvel?*

Elenna frowned as she looked down at the map. "This says that this Beast" – she squinted to read the small, curled script – "Torpix, should be right where we're standing. He must be hiding."

Storm tossed his head and Silver sniffed the ground, giving a small whine.

"We have to stay alert," Tom said. He put away the map and grasped his sword, heaving it from the ground. "It's not just a Beast we face. It could be Malvel, too." He turned to Elenna. "Watch my back, will you?" he asked. "I'm going to try and get through these vines."

"But—" Elenna began.

"I'll be fine," Tom said. "Keep an eye on Petra."

The little witch was watching them carefully. "You know you won't be able to defeat Malvel, don't you?" she called.

Tom shook his head at her. "Haven't you learnt anything?" he asked. "Don't you know when to stop taunting us? We could have defeated you back there, the moment we emerged from the tunnels."

Petra scowled and kicked up dust from the ground. Tom wouldn't let her see that her words had affected him, but still… *Is she right? Have I come this far just to lose a fight against Malvel?*

Tom shook himself and strode right up to the vines. He grabbed one of

the long, snake-like plants. He tried
to pull it to one side so that he could
find a way through.

The vine juddered under his palm,
the thick green surface rippling with
power and strength. The plant next
to it began to shake and twist. Soon
the whole ring of vines was
shuddering violently.

"I don't like this," Tom muttered. He
tried to step back, but the tip of
a vine whipped forward and snaked
around his wrist, cutting into his skin.

"Tom, hold on, I'll get you out,"
Elenna cried, but it was too late. Tom
found himself being dragged into the
writhing mass of green tendrils.

The vines were attacking him!

CHAPTER THREE

DEADLY EMBRACE

"Let me go!" Tom yelled, trying to tear the plants from his limbs. But even more vines lashed out, wrapping around his arms and lifting him high into the air.

"Tom!" Elenna cried, dashing forward.

"No, stay back," Tom shouted, as his brave friend jumped up to try and pull him down. Her fingers closed on thin air and she fell back. Already, the vines had lifted Tom far out of reach.

"I'll go and get Storm!" she gasped.

But before Elenna could move, a thick vine shot down and wrapped itself around her legs.

"No!" she screamed, as she was pulled into the circle of vines. They writhed and hissed. Her body bucked as she tried to kick herself free, but Tom could see the angry coils of vine tightening around her, until she grew still. There was no point struggling – it just seemed to make the vines even more angry.

Silver gave a howl and leapt towards the base of the hedge, snapping at the thick vines with his teeth. He tore at the plant, jerking his head to one side to spit out green chunks, but a twisting coil of vine snapped towards the wolf and he had to leap out of the way.

With a fierce whinny, Storm galloped forwards and kicked out with his front hooves, leaving deep dents in some of the coils.

They oozed clear liquid.

"Storm, watch out," Tom called as the vines tried to snake down and capture the stallion – but Storm was too fast and skittered backwards.

Tom was still suspended high in the air. His ribs creaked with the pressure of the vines' grip and he felt light-headed. He tried not to fight, but it was hard for him to give in to being trapped. Elenna was beside him, her face pale and lips white as she gripped a vine that circled her chest. Her breath came out in shallow, wheezy pants and her eyelids were starting to droop.

"Don't pass out!" Tom called. "Stay awake!" *The Quest couldn't end now. While there's blood in my veins*, he thought, *I'll get us out of here.*

But how? There was no point in

writing and kicking – it only made
the vines grasp him tighter. Instead,
he tried to gently wriggle his body
out of one of the coils.

Elenna noticed what he was doing,
and her eyes lit up. She didn't say
a word, but began doing the same.
Her foot slipped and kicked sharply
against a vine, and Tom saw her bite
her lip with pain as the plant
constricted around her. Tom felt
a vine wrap around his head and
start to tighten over his skull.

Using all of his strength, Tom
managed to drag his sword arm out
of the grip of the killer plant. Holding
the hilt of his sword tightly, he
dragged the edge of his blade along
the vine that grasped his body. He'd
have to be careful not to cut his
own flesh!

A high-pitched screech filled the air and the tendril loosened and dropped away. Tom swung down at the vine that held his stomach and cut it in two. Thankfully, the vine around his head loosened – he was free! The wind whistled past his ears as he fell to the ground and landed with a thump.

Jumping to his feet, he ran at the circle of snake-like plants and, with a fierce cry, hacked at the base of the vine holding Elenna. The vine screamed in pain and swiftly dropped her. She fell to the ground in a heap.

"Thanks," Elenna gasped, and they both staggered backwards as Tom pulled her to her feet.

Tom scanned the area as Storm and Silver came to stand by his side. They were alive, but the Eternal Flame was

still out of reach on the other side
of the huge hedge. How were they
going to get to it?

"Where is that witch?" Elenna
asked. "Surely she knows
something."

"I don't know," Tom replied,
looking around. She'd disappeared.
"But I bet she knew those vines

would attack when we touched them."

Elenna sighed. "If we can't get through the vines then Malvel surely won't be able to, either. The Warlock's Staff may still be safe."

But Tom wasn't so sure. "For now, maybe. But Malvel can use magic."

Elenna looked worried. "What can we do?"

Tom rubbed at his temple. "I just wish I still had my Golden Boots." He looked down at the very ordinary shoes on his feet. "If the golden armour hadn't been returned to my father, I'd be able to jump over those vines in one bound."

Storm nuzzled Tom's neck and Tom felt a grin break out on his face. *Of course!*

During their Quests, Tom had seen

his horse jump great heights – Storm might just be able to leap over the vines and take them to the other side.

He quickly told Elenna his plan.

"Will he be able to make it with both of us on his back?" she asked.

"I think he can, but it will take every bit of his strength," Tom admitted.

"What about Silver?" Elenna asked, her face pale.

Tom's gaze came to rest on the wolf. There was no way Silver would be able to come with them. "We'll have to leave him behind."

Elenna crouched down beside her wolf and gave him a hug. "You'll be our lookout," Elenna murmured into Silver's fur. "At the first sign of Malvel you must howl to alert us.

But don't go near him, Silver – he
can hurt you."

Silver gave a yelp as if promising
Elenna that he would be careful.

Tom climbed into Storm's saddle
and Elenna jumped up behind him.
They led Storm away from the circle
of vines at a trot so that they could
have a good run-up. *I just wonder
what we'll find on the other side*, Tom
thought.

Once they were facing the vines,
Tom snapped Storm's reins.

"Come on, boy," he muttered.

"As fast as you can."

As they galloped forwards, Tom rubbed the fragment of Tagus's horseshoe which was embedded in his shield. It instantly gave them a burst of extra speed. Tom lay low over Storm's neck and squeezed his knees.

"Hold on," Tom cried as the stallion launched upwards, the wall of vines standing impossibly tall in front of them. This was the greatest test of Storm's life!

CHAPTER FOUR

THE SECRET OF THE ETERNAL FLAME

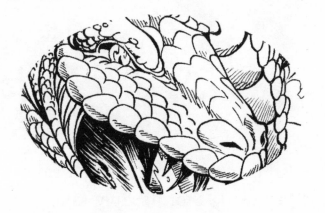

"Come on, boy," Tom cried, snapping the reins that were gripped tightly in his hands. "You can do this."

Storm lifted his head and let out a fierce whinny as he stretched his body to its fullest. Tom and Elenna slammed into the saddle as Storm's hooves cleared the vine wall. They

landed gracefully on the other side.

"Nice work, Storm!" Tom said,
rubbing his horse's sweaty neck.
"You did us proud."

Elenna slipped down from the saddle.
"You are so bra—" She broke off.

Tom looked up to see Elenna
staring open-mouthed at something
directly ahead. He followed her gaze
and gasped as he saw a pillar of

orange and white fire, as tall as
a house, flaring into the blue sky.

"The Eternal Flame," he whispered,
as he quickly dismounted and came to
stand next to Elenna. It was strange,
though – Tom would have expected
the heat from such a huge fire to
make his skin prickle and tighten,
but all he felt was the chill wind.

"I've never seen anything like it
before," Elenna said, shivering as
a fresh breeze passed over them.
"A cold fire?" She glanced round
at Tom, frowning.

"I know," he said. "It must be
some magic special to Seraph."

Tom looked around for signs of
Malvel, but there was no other
person in sight. They'd beaten the
Dark Wizard to the flame! For the
first time in days, Tom started to

relax. Might they be nearing the end of their Quest?

Now we just have to keep Malvel away...

He looked over at his friend. "We need to prepare. Malvel could arrive at any moment. We mustn't let him plunge the Warlock's Staff into the flame."

Elenna yawned and then stretched. "Maybe we should try and steal some sleep."

Tom shook his head. "We can't risk it, we need to be ready. And don't forget – Torpix is somewhere nearby." A prickle of unease passed over Tom. Why hadn't they seen any sign of the Beast?

"We won't be ready for anything if we don't get some sleep," Elenna responded softly. "How can we fight if we're exhausted?"

"But—"

"Tom, it's all right," Elenna said. "Silver is our lookout, and Malvel will have a tough time getting through those vines. We won't be taken by surprise."

Tom thought about it for a moment. His whole body ached and his eyes felt dry with fatigue. Elenna was right – some sleep would do them good.

"All right, he said. "Just for a short while, though."

Tom's chest hurt. He was back in the diamond mines and the walls were closing in on him. The cool rock pressed so tightly he couldn't breathe. He tried to fight it, but it was impossible to move. With a gasp of fear, Tom's eyes snapped open.

Relief surged through him as he saw the dawning sky above. He wasn't in the tunnels – he was on the mountain. At the edges of his vision, he saw the glow from the Eternal Flame. *But why can't I breathe?*

He looked down at his chest and saw the long scaled coil of a snake's body. It was wrapped around him! Torpix! The Beast must have crept up on them in the night. The creature's scales flashed red and gold in the firelight and Tom made out a vicious-looking row of spikes puncturing the Beast's body along its spine. *They'd tear a person apart,* Tom thought. Torpix hissed fiercely as he tightened his hold. He opened his jaws to reveal giant fangs. Tom tried to move but his arms were pinned to his sides.

"Elenna, help me!" Tom croaked, turning his head to try and seek out his friend.

"I can't," gasped a voice.

Tom looked to his left. Elenna had also been by imprisoned by the snake, its long length curling around and around, holding her tight. Her eyes were bloodshot, and her face was mottled and purple.

He heard the clatter of hooves and saw Storm gallop into view. The stallion charged forwards and tried to butt the snake with his head, but the Beast was quicker and struck with its tail, hitting Storm in his flank. The horse dropped to his knees, winded, his eyes glazed with pain.

Tom roared in rage and thrashed wildly. "I won't fail," He gasped. "Not while there is blood in my veins."

Throwing back his head, he looked
right into the eyes of the Beast.
Torpix's head was a flat diamond

shape, his pupils black slits surrounded by red-orange irises that flickered like fire.

Where did he come from? Tom thought wildly. He and Elenna had been alone in the circle of vines when they'd decided to lie down and sleep, Tom had been sure of it. Had the Beast sensed strangers near the Eternal Flame? Had he come to protect the magical cold fire?

Tom couldn't tear his gaze away from the snake's fiery eyes. It was as if he was looking straight into the Eternal Flame... That was it! Cold flames for a cold-blooded animal. "Is that where you came from?" he asked.

The snake tightened his grip and Tom let out a cry of pain as his ribs creaked. It felt as if they were going to crumble at any moment.

Storm snorted and forced himself to his feet as Tom's yell of agony echoed around the circle of vines. With a shake of his mane, the stallion charged fearlessly at the Beast. His lips peeled back as yellow teeth prepared to sink into Torpix's scaly flesh. The Beast turned his body so that the row of barbed spikes were aimed towards Storm. But the clever horse leapt neatly over Torpix and attacked from the rear, sinking his teeth into the scales. The Beast let out a hiss of annoyance and pain. For a moment his body relaxed.

"Now, Elenna!" Tom cried. The two of them managed to slip free and scramble clear.

Tom rolled across the ground and scooped up his sword and shield. He

spun round, ready to face the Beast.

"Watch out!" Elenna yelled.

But it was too late – a steaming jet of liquid flew straight at Tom's face from the snake's hinged jaws hissing and sizzling in the air like acid.

Tom's flesh would be burnt from his bones!

CHAPTER FIVE

THE LAST TOKEN

Tom threw up his shield and heard
a loud sizzle as the liquid hit the
wood, sending out smoke that made
his eyes water.

"Torpix uses acid, Elenna!"
he called over. "Keep yourself
protected."

He ducked his head to get away
from the smoke and spied the lower
part of the giant snake's body. The

Beast's tail seemed to disappear inside the Eternal Flame where its scales took on the colours of the magical fire.

This is the one Beast of Seraph that Malvel didn't create, Tom thought to himself. *Maybe the magical Eternal Flame had created Torpix to protect itself.*

"Tom, are you all right?" Elenna called, getting to her feet.

"I'm fine," Tom insisted. "It's time to defeat this Beast." In trying to guard the fire, the Beast might harm or even kill Tom – and then how would he do battle with Malvel? *I'm sorry, Torpix. I have to do this.*

Holding up his shield so that it covered his face, he charged forwards. Peering over the edge he saw the snake rear up to his full height. His scales glowed in the

light from the fire and the spikes
along his spine looked almost
beautiful as they shone.

Hissss! A jet of acid arced over Tom's
head. Drops began to rain down. In
one fluid movement Tom raised his
shield above his body as a sizzling
rain of acid struck the wood, sending
up a choking plume of smoke.
Tom coughed and spluttered, but

he couldn't stop now.

One foot over the other, he moved closer and closer to Torpix.

"To your left!" Elenna called, warning Tom as the Beast swung his huge body to one side and brought his head around to attack. Tom just had time to leap out of the way and swing his shield around before another jet of acid washed over the wood. More smoke filled the air and flakes crumbled from his shield. He swung his sword out at Torpix's body. The blade bounced off the scales with a spray of sparks, as if he was striking stone.

Tom gave a growl of frustration. The Beast's scales were impossible to penetrate. He swung down with his sword again, painful vibrations going through his arm with the impact,

but his blade left no mark.

Tom stared at the Beast, anger flaring through him. Torpix watched him intently, letting out a long, low hiss. The Beast's head began to sway back and forth. Tom mimicked his action, moving his shield in time with the Beast's swaying, keeping his guard up.

As swift as lightning, Torpix

whipped forwards and lashed out his tongue.

Tom leapt back, just out of reach and Elenna appeared at his side, an arrow strung in her bow.

"Look out!" Tom grabbed her arm and yanked her back behind his shield as the snake's tongue lashed out again. Tom looked down at his most trusted weapon. "My sword can't hurt Torpix. I don't think even your arrows will help this time."

Elenna's eyes were wide with fear as she stared at the Beast. The snake was watching them, his body curled protectively around the base of the Eternal Flame. "If your blade can't harm the Beast, what blade can?"

Tom had an idea. Elenna must have had the same thought because she smiled.

"The last token," they both said at the same time.

Aduro had given them six tokens to help in their fights against the Beasts of Seraph. There was only one token left. Tom remembered the small, sharp knife that lay in Storm's saddlebag.

"We need to reach Storm and get that knife," Tom said.

"What about him?" Elenna asked, nodding her head at Torpix.

"We'll move slowly so that he doesn't attack," Tom replied. "I don't think he likes to be far from the fire."

Elenna nodded. "Let's go."

The two friends edged cautiously over to Storm. Torpix's gaze stalked them across the small clearing, ready to attack at any sudden movement.

"Elenna, hold this for me," Tom

said, handing his sword over to his friend.

"Be quick," Elenna replied. "Torpix looks like he's about to strike."

Tom reached into Storm's saddlebag to take out the knife. It was a little longer than his hand and he felt a wave of nervousness go through him as he held the dagger's hilt. The glass blade reflected the flaring colours of the fire so that it looked like a sharp edge of flame. The tip of the hilt had an emerald jewel embedded into it. *I hope this works,* Tom thought. *It's our last hope.*

"How will you use it?" Elenna asked.

"Torpix's belly is softer than the rest of him," he told her. "It has no scales or spikes."

He saw Elenna looking at the Beast.

She nodded, seeing the vulnerable point – but then she shook her head. "You'll need to get close," she said. "Too close."

Tom weighed the dagger in his hand. "I'll do my best not to wound the Beast too badly," he said. "Just enough to give me time to defeat him."

He turned to face the Beast, but moved too quickly. Torpix shot forth from the flame, crashing to the ground and rearing up in front of Tom. His red and yellow scales glinted in the flickering light of the fire. He opened his jaws wide, acid dripping from his fangs.

Tom charged forwards, ducking and diving as the acid shot out at him. Elenna leapt towards the base of the giant hedge, hoping to find cover there as Storm cantered out of the way. With a single roll, Tom tumbled right up to the Beast. Bending his knees, he leapt upwards in one swift movement. Torpix's tongue lashed out but Tom somersaulted over it and slammed down on the other side of the Beast, sending up a shower of dirt and dust.

As the snake turned to face him, he rose up in fury, exposing his soft, white belly – just as Tom had hoped! He bounded forward, knife raised, and slashed at the underside of the Beast's body, being careful not to sink his blade too far into his flesh.

Torpix gave a hiss of pain, his massive head thrashing from side to side. Tom staggered back in surprise. He hadn't expected the serpent to suffer so much from such a small wound. The Beast's body rippled and swayed as he writhed with agony before he slumped to the ground with a mighty thud. His narrow eyes slowly closed. Tom fell to his knees in front of Torpix's face.

What have I done? he thought.

CHAPTER SIX

THE BELLY OF THE BEAST

Tom watched in amazement as the
wound in Torpix's underside grew
bigger and bigger, as though it was
being pushed open from the inside.
A gush of strange purple blood
spurted into the air. The Beast's head
flapped weakly from side to side as
his hissing turned quiet and faded
away.

Elenna crept closer to the snake. "Tom," she whispered. "Look! Something is crawling out of Torpix's stomach."

"Go and keep Storm at a safe distance," Tom said, getting to his feet and holding the small knife in front of him.

"Sorry, but no," Elenna said. She held Tom's sword in front of her. "Whatever is coming out of that snake, we're fighting it together."

There was a wet, slurping sound as a body surrounded by a thin casing slithered from the snake's stomach. It fell onto the rocky earth with a thump.

Tom peered closer, trying to work out what was in the strange sheath. He heard a low groan as a hand thrust through the slimy casing. It

was followed by an arm, and then...
A familiar face appeared.

Malvel!

The evil wizard climbed to his feet, coughing and spluttering as he freed himself from the slime-bubble. He wiped strands of thick liquid from his face. Torpix dragged his injured body into the heart of the Eternal Flame. The spines on his back hung crookedly to one side as his body and then the tip of his tail disappeared into the cold flames.

Tom stared from the Eternal Flame to Malvel and back again. "What... How...?"

The wizard let out a scornful laugh. "The Beast consumed me – but many thanks, Tom. You set me free!"

Elenna ran forward and pointed Tom's sword at the Dark Wizard.

Malvel glared at her. "Remove that sword from my face."

Elenna shoved the sword forward so that its tip rested under the wizard's nose.

Tom came to her side, brandishing the dagger. He glanced quickly over Malvel's body – he didn't have the Warlock's Staff.

"It's over," Tom said triumphantly. "I'm glad I freed you. That means I can see justice done."

Malvel looked an awful sight, covered in bits of slimy purple membrane. The Dark Wizard curled his lip in disgust, but his smile faltered.

"Your mission is over," Tom said. "Where is the Warlock's Staff?"

Malvel looked up and laughed. "The question you really need to ask yourself is, how could the great hero Tom ruin Seraph?" He gave a cackling laugh. "Don't you see? Look how the vines are dying. They were linked to Torpix – the Good Beast you wounded."

Tom felt a ball of dread in his stomach. He looked around to see that Malvel was right. The circle of twisted vines was blackening and withering before their eyes. Without the vines to protect the Eternal Flame, would Seraph be left open to any attack now?

"It's not your fault," Elenna whispered. "How were you to know?"

"Don't make excuses for me," Tom said sadly. "I was sent here to protect the Eternal Flame and instead I've exposed it to danger."

Tom slammed his shield into
Malvel, knocking him onto his back.
"You made me do this," Tom raged.
"I only wanted to wound Torpix to
get him out of the way so that

I could deal with you!" With a roar, Tom raised his dagger above his head, about to strike.

"Tom, no!" Elenna leapt forward and gripped his arm. "You can't stoop to Malvel's level. We should take him back to Avantia as our prisoner."

Elenna's voice came to him like sunlight through cloud. Tom gasped and dropped his dagger, horrified. Of course it would be wrong to kill the Dark Wizard.

Malvel sprang forward with the speed and power of a cornered animal. He seemed to have regained all his strength, and knocked Tom aside to snatch up the fallen dagger.

Elenna rushed to stop him but, in one fluid movement, Malvel thrust his arm upwards and knocked Tom's sword from her grip. In the next instant he held the blade to her throat. "Time to dance to my tune, Tom," he snarled.

CHAPTER SEVEN

TOM'S CHOICE

Tom kept his gaze trained on Malvel as he picked up his sword. He could hear Silver howling from the other side of the vines, as if the wolf could sense that Elenna was in trouble. Storm joined him with an angry whinny. The animals gave Tom strength, even though Elenna's eyes were wide with terror.

"Let her go," he told the wizard.

"The real battle is between us."

Malvel laughed evilly. "And why would I do a stupid thing like that?" He pressed the blade harder against Elenna's skin. She gave a low sob of pain and squeezed her eyes tight shut. "I think we both know that destroying your best friend would be the best way to destroy you."

Tom could feel his whole body shaking with rage. His eyes felt gritty and hot. "Let her go or you'll be sorry."

Malvel met Tom's stare. "I'll let her go, but only if you help me first."

"What do you want?" Tom demanded.

"The Warlock's Staff has been stolen by my treacherous apprentice." Malvel scowled. "Petra took it just before I was eaten by Torpix. She's probably nearby, waiting for her moment to burn it in the flames herself. Get the Staff from her, and I will let Elenna go."

"Tom, don't you dare," Elenna cried.

What should I do, what should I do? Tom thought. If he tried to get close to Elenna, Malvel could panic and really hurt her. Maybe even kill her.

But I can't let him have the Warlock's Staff either, Tom thought to himself. If Malvel touched the Staff to the Eternal Flame, all would be lost for every kingdom.

Suddenly, something crashed through the vines with a wild growl. Tom swung round, sword held ready. He stopped as he saw Silver charging towards them. The wolf had burst through the blackened vines and was hurtling straight at Malvel, determined to save Elenna.

"Stop him," Malvel cried.

Tom grinned. "How can I reason with a wolf?"

Silver launched himself at the wizard. His jaws dripped saliva and Malvel staggered back, still clutching Elenna to him. But she saw her chance and ripped his arm away, sending the dagger clattering to the ground as she twisted round and sank her teeth into the flesh of his wrist. The wizard cried out in pain and sank to his knees. Silver barrelled into him, sending Malvel's body into the dust. He scrambled away as Silver ran to his mistress.

Tom didn't hesitate. He leapt forwards and kicked the Dark Wizard, who fell back, his head striking against rocks on the ground. Woozy, Malvel tried to sit back up

and fight, but Tom caught hold of his
collar and dragged him towards the
Eternal Flame. The wizard struggled
and shouted, the blood from his head
dripping onto the ground. Tom
tugged him to his feet and stared into
his terrified face.

"You tried to blackmail me and you hurt my friend. More than that, you'd have ruined every kingdom I've fought for. You're going back to the King's dungeon."

Malvel sighed, his shoulders slumping. Tom felt a thrill of hope – was his nemesis finally admitting defeat?

"Never!" Malvel thrust his fists at Tom's face. Instinctively, Tom swung Malvel's body with all his strength, sending him flailing through the air. The Dark Wizard screamed as he stumbled into the Eternal Flame, the dagger still clutched in his hand. He twisted and writhed as the golden fire licked over his robes. He didn't catch alight, but the flames seemed to torture him. He crumbled to the ground then suddenly his cries were

silent. His figure had vanished among
the hungry, flickering flames.

Tom stared at where Malvel had
stood a moment before.

"I wanted to take him back to
Avantia," he muttered. "I wanted to
see justice done." But he knew that
he'd had no choice. If he had not
defended himself, Malvel would have

sent him into the Eternal Flame.

There was a massive explosion of sparks from the Eternal Flame and the fire shot out a jet of rocks. Elenna dived at Tom, pushing him clear.

They tumbled across the ground and Tom lay on his back, trying to catch his breath.

Elenna pulled him into a sitting position. "Are you hurt?" she asked.

"No," Tom said, rubbing the side of his face. In truth, his body was singing with pain but he'd recovered from injuries before and would heal again.

The two friends looked into the Eternal Flame and Silver came to rest beside them. "I wonder if he's really gone?" Elenna asked.

"I don't think there's any way he could survive a fire like that," Tom murmured. "Or Torpix." Had the

Beast been waiting for Malvel?

Tom sighed, his eyes feeling heavy. He swayed with exhaustion as he got to his feet.

Elenna looked at him with concern. "Maybe you should lie down."

Tom felt determination swell inside him. This Quest wasn't over yet. "We need to find the Staff and save Aduro."

Silver suddenly let out a warning howl. There was a crashing sound from the other side of the blackened curtain of vines and a figure emerged.

It was Petra. She held up the Warlock's Staff triumphantly.

"Looking for this?" she asked with a sly smile. "Well, you're too late."

Then she broke out into a run, holding the Staff out before her squat little body. She was going to burn it in the Eternal Flame!

CHAPTER EIGHT

THE GUARDIAN

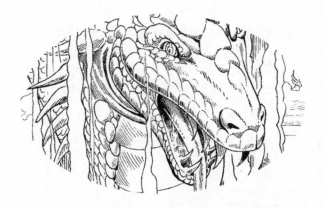

"No!" Tom shouted, as Petra ran towards the flame.

There wasn't time to chase after her. He grabbed his shield and threw it in a low arc. The side of it slammed into Petra's stomach. With an "Oomph!" she collapsed to the ground, the Staff falling from her grasp.

The witch scrambled to her feet,

holding her middle, her face creased with pain. Tom raced forwards and grabbed her by the arm. "This ends now!" he said.

Elenna snatched up the Staff. "I'll look after this."

Petra's eyes narrowed to slits. "You can stop me, but you will still lose. You hurt Torpix and now the vines are dead, and there's no one to protect the Eternal Flame."

"I'll protect it," Tom said. "I'll guard it forever if I have to."

"Tom, no," Elenna said, moving to his side. Silver and Storm came with her. "You can't stay here."

An explosion of sparks from the Eternal Flame filled the air. Tom and Elenna dropped to the ground and covered their heads.

Curling out of the fire, Torpix

appeared. The great Beast loomed over both of them, fangs bared and eyes blazing.

Tom's looked at the Beast's underside, where he had slashed it with the dagger. There was no wound now – not even a scar. The Beast was healed!

Tom stared into Torpix's eyes, which blazed with hate. *If only I could explain that I'm sorry I hurt him and that I'm not his enemy.*

His fingers went to the jewelled belt around his waist. Of course! The red jewel that he'd won from Torgor the Minotaur, which allowed him to communicate with Beasts.

I'm sorry I hurt you, Tom said in his mind. *I was trying to protect the Eternal Flame – just like you.*

Torpix's eyes swept over the figures

standing in front of him, finally
settling on Petra. As though he
recognised evil, he bared his fangs
and with a mighty hiss swooped
down towards her.

Petra screamed. Tom pulled the witch back and stood in front of her. He sent an urgent thought to the Beast: *She's our prisoner. Let us take her and I promise the Eternal Flame will be safe.*

Torpix hesitated, but then seemed to relax. His body slowly coiled back into the Eternal Flame.

Tom heard a creaking sound coming from behind him and turned to see that the twisted vines were growing once again, the withered strands being replaced with new green growth. Tom's heart sank. *How are we going to get through the vines with Silver and Petra?* The plants already stood taller than a house.

Torpix gave a loud hiss, like a command. The vines formed an arch big enough to allow them through.

Tom watched the flames engulf the snake once more. Torpix dipped his head in farewell, the slits of his eyes shining with understanding. Tom felt a swell of pride – he'd made a valuable friend in Seraph, despite their battles.

As Tom led her towards the arch, Petra began to struggle, hitting out at him. "Get off me," she snarled. "I'm not going anywhere with you."

"I just saved your life," Tom snapped. "How about thanking me, rather than punching me in the arm?"

"Never!" Petra said.

Tom shook his head and handed Petra over to Elenna who pushed her through the vines with one hand, leading Storm with the other.

Silver followed, growling at Petra in

case she tried to escape.

Tom picked up his shield before giving Torpix a last look. The Beast could not be seen through the roaring fire of the Eternal Flame but Tom hoped that the serpent could hear him when he sent his final words: *Thank you.*

CHAPTER NINE

THE WAY HOME

On the other side of the vines, Tom could see a hole torn into the air, filled with swirling cloud and light.

"It's a portal!" Elenna exclaimed.

Tom snorted and turned to Petra. "You had it all planned, didn't you? Once you had stolen the magic from the Eternal Flame you were going to make a quick escape to Avantia."

Petra swallowed hard but nodded.

"Come on Tom, we've been through a lot, that has got to count for something." Her voice took on a whining tone. "Please don't take me back to Avantia as a prisoner." Her face became desperate. "Listen, I'll tell you whatever you want to know about Malvel. We can defeat him once and for all, together."

Tom shook his head. "Malvel's gone. You're all out of chances, Petra. We're taking you back."

Tom gazed one last time over Seraph, relieved and proud that order had been restored to this perfect kingdom. *Hopefully evil will never touch Seraph again*, he thought.

He stepped through the portal, with Silver close behind. Tom could feel the wind slapping his face and stinging his eyes. Elenna's hair

whipped all around her head and
when Tom looked round, Storm's tail
streamed out behind him. Energy
crackled in the air and, in an instant,
they were back in Avantia.

They found themselves in a room

lined with swords, battleaxes and longbows. Tom sighed with relief. The portal had brought them back to King Hugo's palace and into the armoury. He smiled. The room had been magically restored to its previous state.

Carrying the Warlock's Staff with care, Tom crossed the chamber. The last time he was here, Aduro had showed him the secret compartment where the Warlock's Staff was normally hidden. Tom's fingers touched the wall, trying to remember what the wizard had done next. He inserted his index finger between two stones, where the mortar had fallen away, and felt a small lever jutting up from between them. He pulled down on it hard. There was a *click*, followed by a *thunk*. The wall opened, becoming a narrow doorway that was as high as his chest. It revealed a small chamber with nothing but a red velvet cushion on a low altar.

Tom knelt down and placed the Staff gently back on the altar on top of the velvet cushion. "Our Quest is finally complete," he murmured. "The Warlock's Staff is back in its rightful home."

Elenna shook her head. "It's not quite finished, Tom – we've got the small problem of a witch apprentice. It's her fault that Aduro disappeared."

Tom nodded, feeling a wave of sadness flow through him. "Aduro may never come back."

Petra began to struggle, but Elenna held on tight, marching her out of the room. Silver followed close at Elenna's heels as Tom led Storm.

As they approached the King's throne room, they spotted a palace guard and servant talking. The guard instantly recognised Tom and Elenna but looked at Petra with suspicion.

"Can we help?" the guard asked.

"Yes," Elenna replied. "This girl is to become a prisoner of Avantia, until her trial."

The guard nodded and took Petra's arm. The witch apprentice didn't even protest. She simply glared at Tom and Elenna.

"Malvel escaped from the dungeon and I will, too," she whispered.

Tom stared her straight in the eye. "If you escape, I'll find you – don't doubt it for a moment." He glanced up at the guard. "Take her, and watch her closely."

The guard bowed his head and led

Petra down the hallway to the
dungeon.

The remaining servant gave a small
cough. "May I be of service?" he asked.

Tom stroked Storm's head and
handed over the reins to his stallion's
bridle. He smiled down at Silver.
"I think these two could do with
some water and hay. Would you

take them to the stables?"

The servant nodded.

"And make sure they rest," Elenna added, giving Silver a swift hug and then ruffling his fur. "They're exhausted."

"I'll see to it," the servant promised, guiding Storm and Silver away.

"Come on," Tom said. "Let's go and report to King Hugo"

They raced to the King's throne room and skidded to a halt as everyone turned to look at them.

The King stood up from his throne, his face creased with concern. "Back so soon?" he asked.

"We finished our Quest, King Hugo," Elenna replied. "The Warlock's Staff is back where it belongs."

"But how can this be?" King Hugo asked, his face a mask of confusion.

"You've only been gone a few hours."

Elenna pointed to the wound Malvel had made at her neck and the bruises that striped her arms from the vines that had tried to crush her. "We've fought hard in Seraph for many days. I have the scars and injuries to show it."

"I don't understand," Tom said. "Why have only a few hours passed here but days in Seraph?"

"It's very simple really," said a familiar voice from by the door. "Time in Seraph moves faster than in Avantia."

Tom whipped round and grinned with relief. Aduro stood in the doorway, a broad smile on his face and a healthy colour in his cheeks.

"You're alive!" Elenna said, her voice filled with happiness.

"Thanks to you two," Aduro
responded. He strode into the room,
his long blue cloak sweeping across
the floor. The Good Wizard smiled at
them. "Now that the Warlock's Staff
is in its rightful place, I can live
again."

"Malvel's gone for good," Tom said.
"He perished in the Eternal Flame."

Aduro's face paled, his lips pressing

into a thin line. Tom felt an icy finger of dread skim down his back. He'd expected Aduro to be pleased, but instead the Good Wizard frowned, his face set along hard lines. "Are you sure about that?"

"No, I'm not sure," Tom stuttered, glancing at Elenna. "I mean, he seemed to disappear—"

"'Seemed' isn't good enough!" Aduro muttered, rubbing a hand across his brow. "Avantia would not have been protected while I was...away."

"Surely this is a time of celebration!" King Hugo boomed. "Malvel, our greatest enemy, has been defeated. We shall have a feast and—"

The king's words petered out as he saw the look on Aduro's face. Then the Good Wizard shook himself and forced a smile.

"You're right," he said. "Let's celebrate." Courtiers cheered and servants ran to the kitchens, ready to bring steaming pots of stew up to the palace dining hall. A mandolin player started to tune his instrument.

Tom and Elenna followed Aduro to a window that looked out over the courtyard.

"Everything will be all right, won't it?" Elenna asked uncertainly. "Tom succeeded in his Quest."

"He did, he did," Aduro muttered.

So why did Tom feel such a knot of uncertainty in his stomach?

The Good Wizard turned to face them, placing a hand each on Tom and Elenna's shoulders. "But I don't know what Malvel could have done to this kingdom while I was away."

Tom's hands balled into fists. "We're always here for you," he said.

"That may not be enough this time," said Aduro, his voice weary. Tom heard Elenna gasp.

"Not enough?" he repeated. "But I've always completed my Quests."

"That's true," Aduro admitted, slapping Tom's back. "You're the bravest young warrior I've ever known." Aduro brought his face close and the next words came out in a whisper. "But your greatest test lies ahead of you."

Whatever Tom had achieved in Seraph, he realised for the first time that it might not have been enough.

Avantia was still in danger.

Join Tom in the *Master of the Beasts*,
his next Beast Quest adventure,
where he will face

NOCTILA
THE DEATH OWL

Win an exclusive
Beast Quest T-shirt and goody bag!

Tom has battled many fearsome Beasts and we want to know
which one is your favourite! Send us a drawing or painting of
your favourite Beast and tell us in 30 words why you think
it's the best.

Each month we will select **three** winners to receive
a Beast Quest T-shirt and goody bag!

Send your entry on a postcard to
BEAST QUEST COMPETITION
Orchard Books, 338 Euston Road, London NW1 3BH.

Australian readers should email:
childrens.books@hachette.com.au

New Zealand readers should write to:
Beast Quest Competition, PO Box 3255, Shortland St,
Auckland 1140, NZ or email: childrensbooks@hachette.co.nz

**Don't forget to include your name and address.
Only one entry per child.**

Good luck!

All books priced at £4.99,
special bumper editions
priced at £5.99.

Orchard Books are available from all good bookshops, or can
be ordered from our website: www.orchardbooks.co.uk,
or telephone 01235 827702, or fax 01235 8227703.

Series 9: THE WARLOCK'S STAFF
COLLECT THEM ALL!

Malvel is up to his evil tricks again! The fate of
all the lands is in Tom's hands...

978 1 40831 316 9

978 1 40831 317 6

978 1 40831 318 3

978 1 40831 319 0

978 1 40831 320 6

978 1 40831 321 3